To the six babies,
with a great deal of love.

LONELY MARIA

Elizabeth Coatsworth

ILLUSTRATIONS BY

Evaline Ness

PANTHEON BOOKS

With this book the author pays tribute
to Vassar College on the occasion of its Centennial.

MARIA

was
a little girl
who lived
all alone
with her
family on a
small island
in the
West Indies.

Her

FATHER

was a
fisherman.
Every day
he went out
in his boat
to tend his
fish traps.

Her

MOTHER

was busy

doing

the work

in

their

HOUSE

which was built of blocks of white coral. Its
roof was made of palm leaves.

At night as Maria was falling asleep she could
hear the palm leaves rustling overhead as
though they were whispering together, but
she could never understand what they said.

Maria's

GRAND
FATHE

was
an
old
man.

Every fine day he sat on a bench outside their house, sometimes in the sun, sometimes in the shade, according to how hot it was. He was always busy making or mending fish nets.

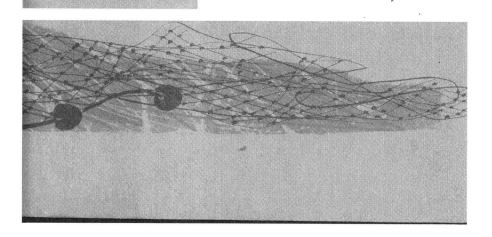

There were no other children on the island. The sea was Maria's only playmate.

It talked with Maria, and at night it sang her to sleep. It sent its waves along the shore to play games with her. It brought her presents of shells. And it gave her the sandy beach all for her own.

Maria loved the beach. She often sat there and drew pictures in the sand with a stick. She

was like her grandfather. She had clever hands.

But one day she grew tired of all her games. She went to her grandfather.

"Grandfather," she said, "I am lonely."

Her grandfather sat and for a long time he looked out across the sea in silence.

Then he said, "I, too, used to be lonely when I went fishing all alone in my boat. But at last I learned that I could make anything happen. I remember how one day my little boat was surrounded by mermaids, all playing on tambourines and Spanish guitars."

"How did you do it, Grandfather?" Maria asked eagerly.

"Everyone must find his own way," said her grandfather.

So Maria went back to her beach and thought and thought and thought, and at last she picked up a stick and drew a picture of a house in the sand.

Thinking of the house, Maria closed her eyes, and when she opened them, a wonderful thing had happened. There stood the house and she could go into it whenever she liked. Then she began to furnish it. For tables she used the crates she found on the beach, and she carried back an old tortoise shell for a seat. A breeze blew through the windows of Maria's house and it was cool, even at noon.

Now the next day, Maria thought that she would like a garden, so she took her stick and drew flowers in the sand. And when she had closed her eyes, up sprang all sorts of beautiful flowers, scenting the air with their sweetness.

But when Maria's father came back from his fishing, he walked past her new house and right through her garden and never saw them.

The next day, Maria took her stick and drew a kitten in the sand and, closing her eyes, said,

"Kitten that I draw today,
Come and play!"

And the next moment, there was the kitten, ready to play! She was colored like the tortoise shell in Maria's house and her eyes were as green-blue as the sea.

Maria
named
her

NINA

On the following day, Maria took her stick and drew a dog in the sand. And when she had closed her eyes and opened them again, the dog stood up and barked. He was a big dog and yellow as the sand.

Maria
named
him

ARLOS

The very next morning, Maria drew a goat in the sand. No sooner had she closed and opened her eyes than the goat bleated. She was as white as the foam of the sea, so

Maria
named
her

LANCA

Now came a day when the wind began to blow and clouds appeared over the sea. Maria knew that a storm would come soon. Quickly she took her stick and drew a horse in the sand, and when she opened her eyes, the horse neighed. He was gray and white like the clouds over the sea, and

Maria
named
him

PINTO

Then Maria climbed on Pinto's back and with Nina in her lap and Carlos and Blanca following, she galloped across the island. She galloped right past her own house, but neither her mother at the window, nor her grandfather mending nets on the bench by the open door, saw her go by.

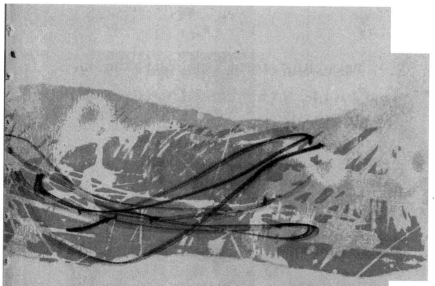

The next day the sea was very rough and Maria's father did not go fishing. When Maria put a shawl over her head to go out, her mother said, "It is too windy, Maria."

"I will be gone only a little tiny minute," promised Maria.

The waves and the wind were very noisy, but Maria, holding tight to the blowing shawl, ran down to see her house and garden and Nina and Carlos, Blanca and Pinto.

"Be careful of them," she said to the waves, and ran back to her house fast, fast, with the wind behind her.

Soon after, came the rain.

All that day the wind and the rain howled across the island, tearing at the palm leaf roof of the house. Fiercely the waves threw themselves far up the shores. But early next morning, when Maria woke, the storm was over and the sun was shining again.

Maria crept out of the house on tiptoe so as not to disturb the others.

But alas! When Maria came to the beach, she found no house, no garden, no Nina, no Carlos, no Blanca, no Pinto! The storm had washed them all away.

Maria thought that her heart would break.

For a long, long time she ran up and down the beach looking and calling for her lost companions. But at last Maria knew that it was no use. The sea had taken them away.

What should she do? Maria turned to go home. But no. That would not help. She came slowly back to the beach. The storm had uprooted a coconut palm. Maria sat down on the smooth trunk and thought and thought.

For a long time she sat there, looking out at the sea.

Then suddenly Maria jumped up. She had made up her mind what to do. Only Maria could help Maria now. She ran along the beach until she found a stick. Then she drew something very fast in the sand. She was frowning. Once or twice she rubbed out what she had drawn with one bare foot, and drew it over again.

When Maria had finished, she stood looking at her drawing and shook her head. She added something and looked again. Then at last she gave a little nod. It would have to do.

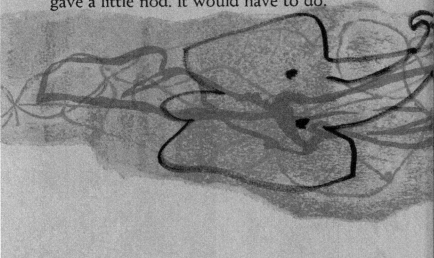

Maria closed her eyes, and when she opened
them what in the wide world do you suppose
she saw standing there on the beach, very large
and very gentle?

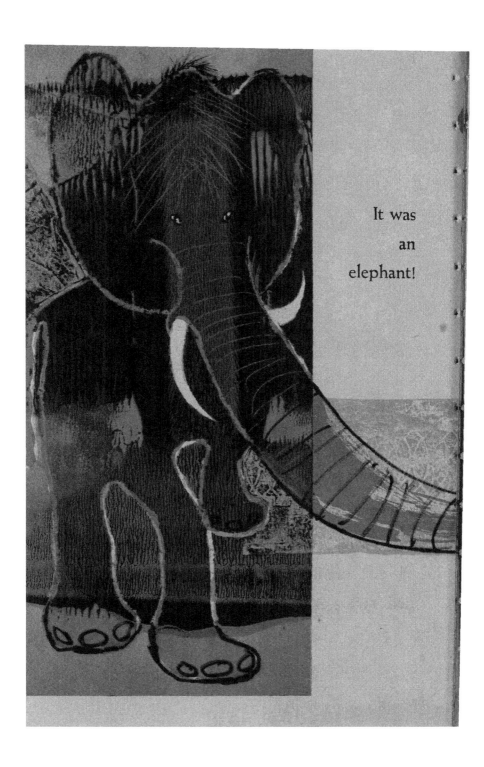

It was
an
elephant!

Perhaps the elephant wasn't quite like other elephants. Maria had seen a picture of an elephant named Jumbo in her mother's old geography, but she hadn't looked at it carefully.

Still, he was very large and grand. And he *was* an elephant. From the moment she laid eyes on him, Maria loved him.

She named him JUMBO

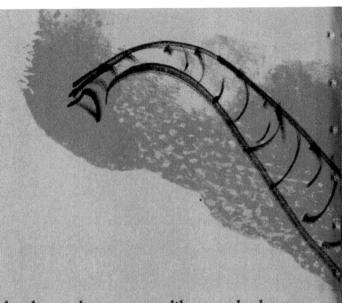

Jumbo knew how to act like an elephant. He knelt down and with his trunk lifted Maria and put her on his head.

From her high seat Maria looked down at her great friend and playmate, the sea, and smiled forgivingly.

"You can take everything away from me, if you want to. I'll be unhappy but I'll start right over again," she said. "If you take Jumbo, I'll make a

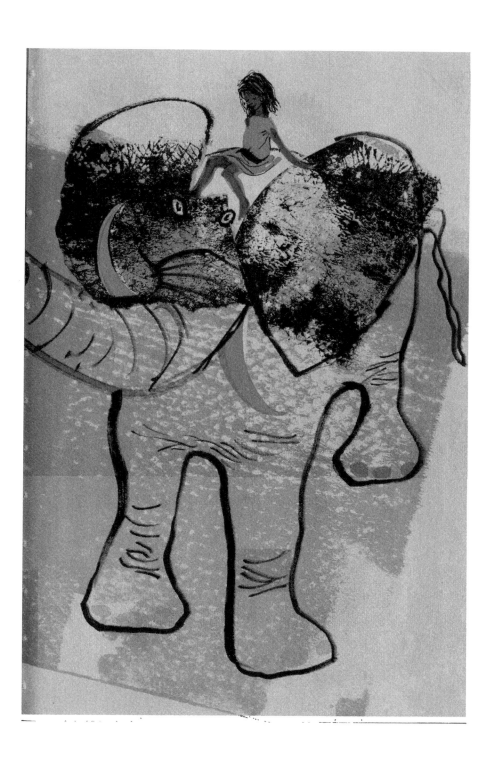

GIRAFFE

with
a red
saddle,

and if someday you take my giraffe, I'll," she
paused to think of the most glorious creature
she could think of, and then said, all in a rush,
"I'll make a gentle
1125345

DRAGON

and
ride
him!

I'll always be able to make *something* wonderful, whatever you do!"

And calling goodbye to the sea, Maria rode off, while all the waves stood on tiptoe to watch her go and waved their white handkerchiefs gaily.

CPSIA information can be obtained
at www.ICGtesting.com
Printed in the USA
BVHW052018090223
658190BV00015B/181

9 781014 210395